MW01049820

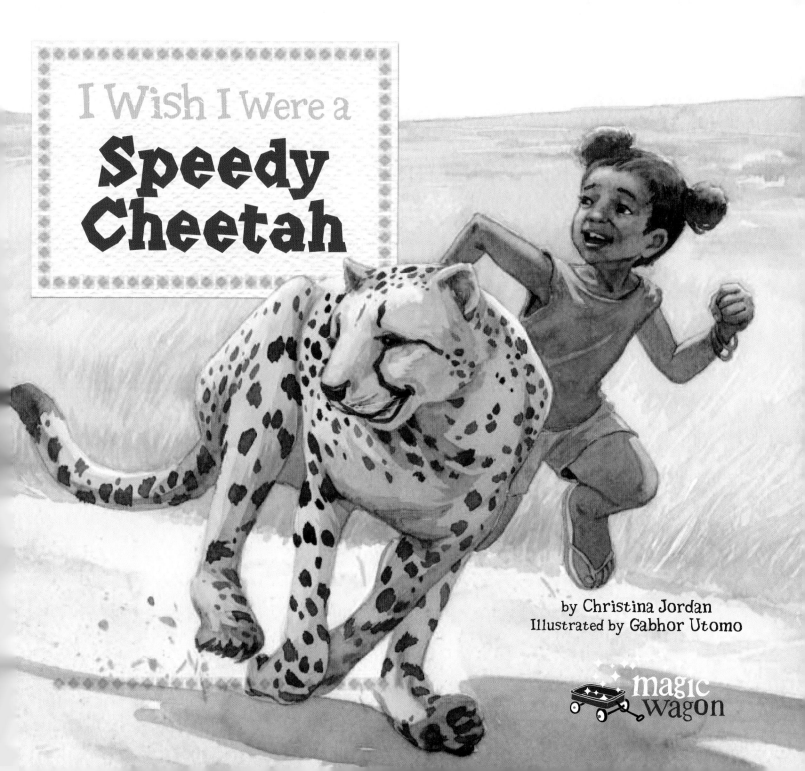

To Kevin, for loving me. — CJ

Published by Magic Wagon, a division of the ABDO Group, 8000 West 78th Street, Edina, Minnesota 55439. Copyright © 2012 by Abdo Consulting Group, Inc. International copyrights reserved in all countries. All rights reserved. No part of this book may be reproduced in any form without written permission from the publisher.

Looking Glass Library™ is a trademark and logo of Magic Wagon.

Printed in the United States of America, North Mankato, Minnesota.
042011
092011

 This book contains at least 10% recycled materials.

Written by Christina Jordan
Illustrations by Gabhor Utomo
Edited by Stephanie Hedlund and Rochelle Baltzer
Cover and interior layout and design by Abbey Fitzgerald

About the Author: Christina Jordan has been an elementary school teacher for 20 years. She also holds a MA in Psychology, is a wife, and a mother of three children. Combining her passion for her profession, education, and her family inspired her to add "author" to her list of accomplishments. The " I Wish I Were . . ." books are Ms. Jordan's first series of children's books.

About the Illustrator: Gabhor Utomo was born in Indonesia, studied art in San Francisco, and worked as an illustrator since he graduated in 2003. He has illustrated a number of children's books and has won several awards from local and national art organizations. He spends his spare time running around the house with his wife and twin daughters.

Library of Congress Cataloging-in-Publication Data

Jordan, Christina.
  I wish I were a speedy cheetah / by Christina Jordan ; illustrated by Gabhor Utomo.
     p. cm. -- (I wish I were--)
  Summary: A young girl imagines how different her life would be if she were a cheetah.
  ISBN 978-1-61641-660-7
  [1. Stories in rhyme. 2. Cheetah--Fiction.] I. Utomo, Gabhor, ill. II. Title.
  PZ8.3.J7646Iav 2011
  [E]--dc22   2010048718

I wish I were a speedy cheetah, the fastest land animal I would be.
My life would be much different than it is just being me.

My home would be on the African savanna, among the tall grass.
This would help keep me camouflaged as my prey would pass.

Unlike my other big cat friends, I would only hunt by day.
But I could sprint 70 miles per hour and not much could get away.

No one would ever pick me very last to play any game.
My speed and quick reflexes would earn me spots in the hall of fame.

My three-mile walk from school each day would quickly go right by.
'Cause as a speedy cheetah, it would seem like I could fly.

Walking miles to gather water to cook and wash each day would no longer be necessary. That chore would go away.

13

But if I were a speedy cheetah some things would have to end, like hanging out in my village and playing footie with my friends.

15

Colorful bracelets or a beautiful dress I could no longer wear.
Instead my clothes would be a coat of spots and golden hair.

I don't think I would like it if my meals were only meat.
I like cassavas, rice and beans, and bananas that taste sweet.

And at night in the savanna with only stars above my head,
there would be no sisters or cousins to sleep next to me in bed.

Oh, speedy cheetah, it would be so great to be as fast as you can be.
But for now, I like who I am. I think I'll just stay me.